For Izzy, who really, REALLY
likes video games

BAD KITTY

Does NOT Like
VIDEO GAMES

NICK BRUEL

A NEAL PORTER BOOK
ROARING BROOK PRESS
New York

Kitty loves this video game. This is her favorite video game. It's about a bunny who jumps over fences and grabs carrots.

Kitty has been playing
this game for five hours.

Stop playing this game, Kitty!
You have to do something else.

If you play outside, draw a picture, and read a book, then you can play your video game again.

No, Kitty! You have to play outside first.

Kitty does not want to play outside.
Kitty wants to play her video game.

Now that she is outside,
Kitty pretends she is a bunny.
Kitty is very good at jumping.
JUMP!

Kitty pretends the leaves are carrots. Kitty is very good at grabbing. **GRAB!**

Now Kitty wants to
play her video game.

No, Kitty! You have to draw a picture first.

Kitty does not want to draw a picture.
Kitty wants to play her video game.

First, Kitty draws a picture of
a bunny grabbing carrots.

But then Kitty draws a **MONSTER** bunny grabbing **MONSTER** carrots.

That is a good drawing!
Now Kitty wants to play her video game.

No, Kitty! You have to read a book first.

Kitty does not want to read a book.
Kitty wants to play her video game.

The book is about a bunny who sneaks into a garden to grab carrots.

Oh, no! There's a farmer!
The farmer chases the bunny!

WHEW!
That was an exciting book!

You played outside. You drew a picture. You read a book. Now you can play your game again, Kitty.

Kitty does not like
video games.